FIRST LOVE

Book # 1

"Samantha's
LOVE & ROMANCE"™
Series

By

Denise Daniella Darcy

Published by
Durango Publishing Corp.®

Acclaim for Denise Daniella Darcy and *FIRST LOVE*

Also by Denise Daniella Darcy

Samantha's LOVE & ROMANCE Series

<u>First Love – Book 1</u>

<u>Rebound Love – Book 2</u>

Coming soon!

<u>Cowboy Love – Book 3</u>

Casual Love – Book 4

Available at:

www.DurangoPublishing.com

www.DeniseDaniellaDarcy.com

&

Amazon

FREE BONUS – ALTERNATE ENDINGS

Hi Readers, Denise here. I just wanted to let you know that I have an unexpected bonus for you. I have written 2 alternate endings for *FIRST LOVE,* and they are yours free.

Why, you may ask? Simple. I always strive to give more than the anticipated, more than the normal. Both endings dramatically change the outcome and are real page-turners.

Get your FREE copy now at:

http://www.denisedanielladarcy.com/firstlovealternates

Just my way of giving you something extra and thanking you for reading my books.

I am busy writing more stories about Samantha's adventures in love so check my website www.DeniseDaniellaDarcy.com for the most up-to-date list. Or just get my newsletter to stay on top of new developments at:

http://www.denisedanielladarcy.com/newsletter

Happy reading -

Denise Daniella Darcy -
"Triple D to my friends"

PS. And as an added SPECIAL BONUS, at the end of this story I have attached a SNEAK PREVIEW of *REBOUND LOVE*, Book 2 in the series. Enjoy!

FYI - The stories in *Samantha's LOVE & ROMANCE Series* can be read in any order. The stories are linked but each one is a separate story. Research has shown that most readers do prefer to read them in sequence.

Other Titles By Durango Publishing Corp.®

Health, Fitness & Dieting Series

YOUR 'Lose Weight FAST the Natural & Healthy-Way DIET', a simple healthy weight loss diet so YOU can live a better, happier, more enjoyable life!

Betting and WINNING Horse Races Series

Horse Racing: Gambling to Win

Vegas Pro's Best Racing Angles

Available at:

www.DurangoPublishing.com

www.DeniseDaniellaDarcy.com

&

Amazon

Table of Contents

Chapter 1 -- Coffee and a cold

shower 11

Chapter 2 -- Uncle Ty 18

Chapter 3 -- Jail time 22

Chapter 4 -- Coconut shampoo..28

Chapter 5 -- Another cold shower

....38

Chapter 6 -- Flip flops and shorts

....46

Chapter 7 -- Haunted house 55

Chapter 8 -- Freak show 61

Chapter 9 -- First time 69

Chapter 10 -- A swift retreat......78

Chapter 11 -- Confrontation 87

Chapter 12 -- Finally, a hot shower

....94

Chapter 13 -- Going for the jugular
....102

Sneak Preview of REBOUND LOVE,
Book 2....................................107

Chapter 1 -- Erotic yoga 107

Chapter 2 --Hong Kong convention
....118

Chapter 3 -- Tom the sound guy
....125

Chapter 4 -- Mixed feelings......132

Chapter 5 --EARTHQUAKE!!.....140

Chapter 6 -- Together with Tom
....148

Recommended Reads 156

About Denise Daniella Darcy....157

First Love

Chapter 1 -- Coffee and a cold shower

Seth's fingers dug into her shoulders as he drew her under the empty bleachers by the football field. The tiny, pleated skirt of her cheerleading uniform lifted in the breeze and she tried unsuccessfully to smooth it down with one hand. The other hand was tangled in Seth's unruly hair. She drew his face to hers and when their lips met she felt heat rising up all through her body.

She wanted him so badly.

Ever since she'd first seen him as a freshman in Mr. Jennings's math class. She'd almost failed, because who could pay attention to Pythagorean Theorem when the boy of your dreams is sitting one seat up and one seat to the left of you?

She'd never even dreamed he felt the same way, but now his hands were drifting downward. He lifted up the little pleated skirt and found she wasn't wearing panties underneath.

He chuckled and gave her a little spank, which stung. Then he grabbed her bottom and ground her against his hips. She could feel his erection between them and it excited her. She felt bold and wicked.

She snaked her hands under his shirt and felt the muscles of his chest. Her fingers grazed his nipples and he responded with more fierce kisses on her neck.

He unzipped her little vest with the school's mascot on the front and exposed her bare breasts. Her nipples crinkled in the breeze. She took his hand and placed it on her breast. He squeezed it and she moaned with delight. The aching pleasure of it drove her wild.

His hungry mouth found her other nipple and he grazed it with his teeth. She shivered. "I need you," she gasped.

She didn't know exactly how he did it but one moment they were standing, pressed together, and the next moment he had her down on the ground. Her skirt was pushed up and she could feel the cool grass under her skin, see the sky through the bleacher seats above her.

Seth pulled off his clothes and stretched himself out on top of her. A kind of electric feeling passed between them everywhere their skin touched, especially where his cock was pressed against her mound. She lifted her hips and pressed impatiently against him. He nibbled her neck once more, and his breath made the hairs on the back of her neck prickle. She pressed hard into him. "Finally…" she whispered.

Seth pulled back and looked her in the eyes. His expression was intense, his gaze fiery. Leaning forward, he pressed his soft lips against her ear and shouted "BEEP BEEP BEEP BEEP BEEP BEEP!"

Ugh... Sam jerked upright, heart pounding. The hell? Oh. She smacked her alarm clock into silence and flopped down onto her pillow again, defensively pulling the down comforter over her head. Seth again. Why was it always him? He'd never actually even touched her, or been in a relationship with her. Or talked to her besides that one time when he needed a number 2 pencil for a test. She hadn't even seen him since graduation. Nevertheless, he had a tendency to show up in her dreams. The kind of dreams that made her want to go back to bed. Stupid alarm.

She rolled out of bed and padded into the kitchen corner of her studio apartment to start the coffee. She'd had it since moving to Buffalo to work for Uncle Ty shortly after graduation. By now she could have found something bigger and nicer, but she was fond of the place. She wasn't in too big of a hurry to move out of her very first apartment.

She showered while the smell of coffee filled the apartment. Her mind drifted back to her dream. If only she could have slept in just a few more minutes! Her soapy hands swept over her breasts, which were full and round, and especially sensitive this morning. One hand reached back and grabbed her butt, hard, like Seth had done in her dream. She felt a tingle starting between her legs, much warmer than the cool shower water.

The coffee timer went ping! and Sam groaned. She always slept in as late as she could, leaving her no time to dawdle, or do other things, in the morning. Uncle Ty liked to get as much work as possible done early so he could leave after lunch if he wanted to. I'm just gonna be extra cranky today, I guess. She rinsed off quickly and wrapped her hair up in a towel, filled a mug with coffee (cream and Splenda), and grabbed some clothes. Luckily, work was almost always casual. She had one suit for meetings, but most of their clients also seemed to prefer jeans and tee shirts. She had no idea where Uncle Ty found them, but it sure made work a lot nicer. She pulled on jeans with flare legs, which she knew were hopelessly out of fashion but she liked how they balanced out her figure and a black tank top and inspected herself in the mirror.

What she saw was a girl of average height and slightly heavier than she would have liked. The tank top clung to the swell of her breasts and the jeans didn't seem to be doing anything to make her bum look smaller. Her hair was longish and brownish and her eyes, behind their emo plastic frames, were big and dark. She would kill a man to be slender, athletic, and blonde.

Instead, everything about her was soft, curvy, and dark. Even her hair tumbled around her face in big fat curls. She pulled on an oversized hoodie, also black, and zipped it up. The morning would be chilly, and the office would be air conditioned. She sipped her coffee while she applied a bare minimum of makeup and pulled back her unruly hair, then headed to the office.

Chapter 2 -- Uncle Ty

Morgan Advertising was a one-man firm located near Main Street downtown. Well, one-man and Sam now. Uncle Tyrone Morgan had run the place himself for basically forever, but had hired Sam after high school so she could get out of her parents' house.

Sam's mom and dad loved her dearly, and did not understand her at all. Being the oddballs of the family, Sam and Uncle Ty were very close.

He was also teaching her to run the business. She had started out as a general flunky and go-fer, but had been gradually accepting more and more responsibility while still having to do all her go-fer duties like making coffee, cleaning up, and getting take-out. She normally left the office feeling a little crazy, but it was also really fun to work for Uncle Ty.

As usual, she arrived first, started a pot of coffee and, as it was Wednesday, started trying to get the filing back in order.

Uncle Ty had a very energetic approach to business that made his office look like it had a poltergeist; much of Sam's grunt work involved the constant battle to restore order.

She was replacing the file for the Ed's Appliances account, which for some reason had been stuck under the goldfish tank, when her uncle strolled in. He was a tall attractive man, starting to go gray at the temples. He was also dressed casually, but always gave the impression that he was wearing a designer suit.

"Good morning!" he sang out, flinging his briefcase in the general direction of his desk.

Sam was still feeling flustered and cranky, but it was hard to stay miffed when

Uncle Ty was feeling self-congratulatory. And he normally was. "Have a good night?" Sam asked.

"The very best of nights, my favorite niece. Twice." He pantomimed snapping imaginary suspenders with pride.

"Poor Deliah. She must be tired"

"Who? No, Robyn is quite energetic. I think I'll keep her."

Sam snorted. No woman had every held Uncle Ty's attention longer than a week. "Where do you keep finding them in a city this small? I would have thought you'd run through the entire female population by now." She handed him his coffee, "Twice."

He tossed his head back and laughed. They got to work.

At lunchtime Uncle Ty declared he was going to step out, in a tone of voice that implied he would not be stepping back in for the rest of the day.

Sam guessed he had plans with the energetic Robyn. "Whatever," she said, "I'll hold down the fort. Once I've gotten through the e-mail I'll get in touch with Mr. Abercrombie. Then I'll tell Mrs. Anderson where she can stick it." She caught his look and corrected herself, "I'll politely tell her where to stick it. Oh, and I'm ordering pens. I can't work without pens." Uncle Ty, who in all other respects was so calm it was hard to find his pulse, was a ruthless dictator when it came to the office supplies budget. "Anything else?"

"I think that's it. Enjoy your afternoon, I know I will!" He swept out.

Chapter 3 -- Jail time

Sam finished the e-mails, contacted Mr. Abercrombie, politely told Mrs. Anderson where she could stick it, and decided to stay late to organize all of Uncle Ty's notes for the next day. When she was done it was five o'clock and she was starving. She decided to get dinner at the restaurant a block down the street before she went home.

The hostess had seated her before she realized she'd forgotten her book. And her phone, her wallet, her keys, and her purse. "Damn!" she muttered, just as the bemused server arrived. "I'll be right back, all right?" blushing, she slunk out of the restaurant.

Luckily, or maybe unluckily, she forgot things a lot. The office door locked automatically, so Sam had figured out how to jimmy open the bathroom window in the back. There were three cinderblocks stacked under it, so she could climb in.

She was halfway through the window, feet first, when she heard gravel crunching in the driveway behind her and the WHOOP WHOOP BLERRT of a police siren. She jerked in surprise and lost her handhold on the window frame. She caught herself just before she fell out, but was now tipped precariously backwards with her back bent painfully over the windowsill.

Upside down, she watched as two policemen approached, flashing their badges. She caught their eyes on her chest, and was uncomfortably aware that she'd taken off her hoodie to fit through the tiny window easier. Her breasts were now threatening to fall out of her tank top.

Embarrassment and rage flooded her.

"Miss, I'm going to have to ask you to come down from there. Keep your hands where we can see them and no sudden movements," said the taller and somewhat older cop.

In her mind, Sam named him Officer Douchecanoe. The younger one, Officer Numbnuts she decided, rested his hand on the butt of his gun and shifted his muscular body, trying to look threatening. The effect was somewhat ruined by his golden curls, angelic face and baffled expression. He looked like a male stripper pretending to be a cop more than an actual officer of the law.

"You know, I don't think it's actually possible to do all that at the same time. You're going to have to pick one or we'll be here all night," Sam snapped. She was scared and annoyed. What the hell was going on?

Douchecanoe frowned and finally looked her in the eye. Numbnuts stepped forward. "Keep your hands where we can see them, and I'll lift you down," he said.

"Yeah, right. Because I want you to ogle me and touch me. Not today, bud-HEY!"

With one arm around her shoulders and the other under her back, he scooped her up and out of the window. Sam could feel the muscles in his arms flexing as he swung her around and deposited her safely on the ground. He smelled like coconut shampoo. For a moment she stood where she was, looking up into his eyes. In the sunset glare she couldn't tell what color they were. He put a big hand on her shoulder and her heart thumped.

He spun her around and pressed her against the side of the police car. "Hey!" she shrieked again.

"Hands on the car, now!" Barked Douchecanoe, in an I-have-a-weapon tone of voice.

Sam complied, her hands were shaking and her knees felt weak. They got weaker as Numbnuts frisked her. He did a very thorough job, his hands lingering here and there, and especially there. When he was finally done he stepped back and Douchecanoe commanded her to turn around.

"Explain what you're doing here tonight," he said. He seemed to be a tiny bit more relaxed now. Maybe being creepy jerks is just how cops make friends, Sam thought.

She explained about her job, and her purse, and that she broke into the office literally once a week. The officers' stony expressions didn't change. "Just call my uncle and he'll tell you," she finished lamely.

"You'll get a phone call from the station," Numbnuts replied, then he spun her around again. You could just tell me, Sam thought, and then she felt the handcuffs click into place.

Chapter 4 -- Coconut shampoo

"Cuffed by a sexy cop! That's too good," Isabella Flores laughed the next afternoon.

"It's not funny," Sam grumbled.

"Ever on the lookout for criminal boobies!"

"They read me my rights. I got fingerprinted. I was in a jail cell."

"You have the right to remain sexy..."

"Oh my god, shut up!"

Isabella didn't stop laughing but she tried to stifle it, and waved for Sam to finish her story. Sam stuck her tongue out at her and continued.

"So, what happened was Uncle Ty had a security system installed and forgot to tell me. I triggered a silent alarm that called the two jerkiest cops in the city."

Isabella leaned back and put her feet up on Sam's desk, her long legs crossed. Tall, willowy, with pale blonde hair, Sam's best friend could have been a model but she was a courier. She stopped by Morgan Advertising several afternoons a week, officially for work, unofficially to hang out.

Their friendship was based on affectionate bickering and absolute trust. Sam had been too plain and shy to have many girlfriends before Isa, and Isa's former friends had been too shallow to hold her interest or jealous of her looks and vivacious personality. Nothing happened to one of them that the other didn't hear about and tease her over.

"I don't know Sam, I think you're lucky you didn't get pepper spayed or beaten up. You probably got the only two decent cops in the city."

"Maybe," Sam conceded. "But they're still dicks."

"Admit it; you're totally in love with Numbnuts."

Sam blushed furiously. "His name is Aiden Williams." Isa laughed again and Sam glared at her. "And I never want to look at him again."

She tried not to think about how it had felt to be held in his arms. *Get a grip, Sam! You are not Bella Swan.* She resolved to change the subject, and the visitor doorbell rang, as if in answer to a prayer. It was probably someone lost. No customers were scheduled to come in today, but a lot of people who were looking for Morgan's Bar and Grill wound up at Morgan Advertising by mistake.

Sam didn't care, it was a distraction right when she needed one.

She pulled open the door and Aidan was right in front of her, last night's hoodie in his hands. His eyes were blue.

Sam froze. She could feel her face getting hot and she had no idea what to do with her hands. For that matter, she had no idea what to do with her whole self. Do something! Say something or shut the damned door. Oh god, he probably thinks I'm an absolute moron. Wait, why should I care?

Aiden smiled down at her. He held out her hoodie, "I wanted to return this to you. You forgot it at the station, and uh..."

From behind her, Sam heard Isa call out, "Could that be officer Williams? How crazy, we were just talking about you. Come on in!" And she nudged Sam out of the doorway, making a flamboyant gesture for Aiden to enter the office.

Sam shot her an incredulous look and she winked.

Aiden stepped past them and looked around the small office, taking in the random piles of filing, the dartboard, and the goldfish with a little smile.

Now that he was inside, he didn't seem to know what to do next so he carefully folded the hoodie and laid it on a chair like it was here for an appointment.

To keep her hands busy, and to try and calm down, Sam started grabbing random folders and jamming them into the filing cabinet.

Never one to allow a lull in conversation, Isa spoke up, "It's nice to meet you. Mind if I call you Aiden? Sam was right, you are hot."

Just kill me now, Sam thought. She turned her back on them entirely, to hide her face.

"How did you decide to be a police officer? Are you a modern day knight in shining armor?" Isa cooed.

Is she flirting with him?

"You could say that. I got into the force because I wanted to help people."

"A killer smile and a heart," Isa stepped closer, Sam turned enough to see her grin up at him. "Aren't you something?"

She is! Jeez she works fast. A sick ache grew in Sam's chest as she watched Aiden and Isa.

They looked so beautiful, standing together, they looked like they were made for each other. Aiden was responding to Isa's flirting, laughing at anything she said, and watching her intently as she moved about the room, first gesturing elegantly then laying a familiar hand on his arm.

Sam's embarrassment died away. Now all she felt was sick and miserable. She realized that she really had been attracted to Aiden, and for a brief moment his coming here had made her think he was interested in her, too.

Hope had been brief but brilliant and its death pierced her heart. She'd been stupid to think there was anything there. A guy like him wouldn't even think of a girl like her.

She let the files drop from her hand and crossed the room, Isa's chipper voice was muffled by the blood rushing in her ears. Listlessly she pulled on the hoodie and zipped it up.

Her movement seemed to break some kind of spell. Aiden's gaze moved to include both of them and he said, 'Well, I'm glad to see that back with its owner. I, uh, I should get going."

Sam mumbled "Yeah, thanks." And Isa waved him out the door.

When she turned back to Sam, she furrowed her delicate eyebrows. "You okay, Sam?"

"Oh sure. I guess I'm just tired."

For a second Isa looked like she was going to call Sam out on her lie, but then she flashed a huge grin and said, "Of course you are. I've got to scram, so you can have some peace and quiet, 'kay?" And she was gone before Sam could respond.

Sam was left alone in the empty office. She hugged her hoodie close around her. She wanted to cry, or break something. It felt like an enormous, cosmic joke at her expense, that the first guy she'd wanted in years would be swept away by her best friend.

The worst part was that she couldn't even be mad, they seemed so right for each other. She imagined Isa catching up with Aiden on the street and it killed her. They would both smile, make plans to go out together, and forget all about her.

She was half right.

Sam went home early for once. She was relieved to shut her door on the whole damned world for a while. She played video games and had a glass of wine.

Her cat, Deadpool, deigned to sit on her lap and purr for a full twenty minutes. It would have been a good night if only she could have stopped thinking about Aiden's blue eyes, his muscular body, the smell of coconut shampoo. Eventually she gave up, set her alarm and changed it from that horrible beep to an upbeat song, and passed out

Chapter 5 -- Another cold shower

Aiden crept into her bed and cuddled up close to her. "Are you awake?" he whispered, dropping a little kiss on her cheek, then her earlobe.

"Mmmmm," she murmured. "I am now." She rolled around to face him. He tangled his hands in her thick hair, pulled her face to his and kissed her deeply. She surrendered her mouth to his insistent tongue and ran her hands along his body. His skin was smooth with a sprinkling of delicate hair on his chest. She loved the feel of his body. He was warm and his muscles moved under his skin in fascinating ways. When she ran her hand across his hip and down to his inner thigh he shivered.

A mischievous look crossed his face. With one hand he pressed her back against the mattress and disappeared under the covers. Sam gasped as she felt him part her legs. His lips pressed against her thighs.

She hadn't had any idea she was so sensitive there. She could feel every tiny move he made as he licked and nibbled, working slowly higher. She sighed happily when he got to the top of her thigh and she felt his finger part her lips.

His tongue was hot and wet. It grazed over her sex, sending waves of sensation through her whole body. She dug her fingers into the mattress, her back arching. "Oh, oh my god!" she gasped. Encouraged by her excitement, Aiden worked her with his tongue even harder, and sucked gently on her lips.

Sam's legs shook involuntarily. Her pleasure was building so powerful and so fast she could barely believe it. She writhed and flexed as his mouth ravished her slit. "Aiden. Oh, I'm..." And then the feelings of pleasure exploded. The climax rocked her and for a moment she was lost in the feelings that throbbed and pulsed though her loins.

Aiden straddled her. He ran his fingers over her nipples, trailed them up her neck and buried them in her hair again. "You're so beautiful," he whispered and slid inside her.

Sam moaned as he filled her. He was so big she was shocked he didn't hurt her, but then, she was so wet and so very ready for this. He thrust into her and she rose to meet him. As they fell into rhythm he caught her wrists and brought them up over her head, watching her face and the movement of her body intently.

Playfully, Sam tried to resist him, but when she pushed against his hands she might as well have been trying to move a brick wall. With a thrill she realized at this moment she was completely in his power. She tightened around him, feeling herself building to another climax.

She thrust harder and Aiden drove himself deep and fast into her. His passion was reaching its peak, and the thought sent another jolt of sensation through her body.

Aiden thrust into her faster and faster, his fingers biting into her pinned wrists. She bucked underneath him, the wetness and the heat and the feeling of his cock plunging inside her was so good. His body jerked and he buried himself deep and hard as he came. She screamed wordlessly at the same time, convulsing beneath him, overcome by the ecstasy rippling through her.

Still inside her, Aiden took a deep breath and said "SO RAISE YOUR GLASS IF YOU ARE WRONG IN ALL THE RIGHT WAYS!"

The alarm clock hit the wall with a crunch. Sam swung her legs off the bed and tried to get a handle on her thoughts.

Judging from how wet she was and the lingering tingle, at least one of those O's had been the real thing. Her heart fluttered. If dream Aiden is that good, how good is the real thing?

She wondered what it would be like to play out her dream in real life. Or spend an entire day in bed with him. Or have him push me up against a wall like he pushed me onto that police cruiser and take me hard...whoa. I need a shower. A cold, cold shower.

As the icy water hit her she remembered yesterday. Aiden and Isa talking like she wasn't there. Obviously too into each other to care if she was in the room. Isa running out after him. She turned the faucet to hot water, not needing to be chilled any more than she already was.

At the office, Uncle Ty gave her a long look. "Kiddo, if you type any more viciously the keyboard's going to burst into flames and we'll need even more pens. Just tell me it's not me you're pissed at."

Sam sighed. She had been taking some comfort in the decisive snap and click of the keys under her fingers, but technology abuse wasn't the answer. "Sorry, Uncle Ty. I'm just feeling frustrated today or something. It's not you." She gave him the best smile she could manage.

"Your mom didn't call, did she?" On the infrequent occasions when Sam's mother called, she tended to unburden herself of her worries about Sam's weight, not going to college, lack of a boyfriend, and general failure to be the ideal daughter. It put Sam in

Denise Daniella Darcy

a foul mood for the next 24 hours and Uncle Ty knew to beware.

"Heh, no. It's nothing. Really."

"All right." Uncle Ty also knew when not to push, but he continued to look concerned. "Tell you what, how would you like to go on a trip for me this weekend? If I can swing it, that is. Mr. Kodama is going to be in the States and if the timing works out he'd like a face to face meeting to talk about strategy and designs for the next few months. You can handle it."

Sam thought. It might be really nice to get away. Business trips for Uncle Ty were always about 40 minutes of work snuck into two or three days of vacation. "Well, I was going to put in some overtime here, but..."

"It can wait, besides, if I know you're not going to come in unexpectedly, I can bring Crystal here to break in my new desk."

A faraway look crossed his elegant face and he ran his fingers across the smooth walnut surface, as if he could already picture sweeping all the supplies off it to make room for another conquest.

"Oh god! I did not need to hear that! Fine, I'll go if it will make you stop. Jeez." She resumed typing, taking care to be gentler. After a few minutes she looked up. "Thanks Uncle Ty. Crystal?"

Uncle Ty grinned wolfishly and sketched an extremely curvy hourglass shape in the air. Sam shook her head.

Chapter 6 -- Flip flops and shorts

Later in the day, Sam was placing some orders by herself, Uncle Ty having excused himself early again, when Isa came in. Sam was relieved to note that, though she still felt jealous and hurt, she was nevertheless as genuinely glad to see her friend as ever.

Unfortunately she also felt tongue tied.

Normally she would tell Isa all about how she was finally attracted to someone, and how monumentally unfair it was that a glamorous other woman had snatched him away. And Isa would find a way to make her laugh about it, and things would be a little better. But Isa was the glamorous other woman and that made things awkward.

Isa seemed to have no such compunctions. "I got three free passes to the

fair tonight. You have to come with us!"
Us? I was right, they're an us. Uuugh.

"I don't want to be in the way, Isa."
Or watch you guys kiss. She pictured sitting
alone on one side of the Ferris wheel bucket
while Aiden and Isa swapped spit across
from her and it made her feel physically
sick.

"Samantha Jane Morgan, I am not
taking no for an answer. Remember
Thanksgiving?"

Sam did remember Thanksgiving.
She had brought Isa to her family dinner,
mercilessly using her as a human shield
because if there was one person her parents
understood less than Sam, it was Isa.

Uncle Ty counted too, but over the
years Sam's Dad had given up on ever
changing his brother so her mom had to give
up too. The meal could have won a

Guinness World Record for "most awkward event of all time."

Especially when Sam's mom tried to compensate by complimenting Isa, saying that with her good looks her pixie cut hair didn't look at all mannish or wrong.

Isa definitely had a favor coming.

"Whatever. But you're really strange, you know. Most girls would want to be alone with the hot boy."

"You're strange Sam. You're my friend is why I want you to come. And Aiden wants you to come too. It's gonna be awesome, you'll see."

Sam bit her lip. Part of her intensely wanted to see Aiden again, but the rest of her knew it was going to absolutely suck to have him in front of her but out of reach.

There was no question of going, though. If Isa was calling in the

Thanksgiving disaster favor then she was dead serious.

She agreed to meet them at 5:00 and Isa graciously allowed her to change the topic to who was most likely to die next in their current favorite show. She managed to feel completely normal around her friend until Isa left, reminding her not to be late to meet them that night, Oh joy.

A few hours later Sam paced around her apartment in her bra and panties. Every piece of clothing she owned was strewn across the floor and the bed, Deadpool "helping" her by threading himself around her ankles and dropping hair on everything.

Her usual jeans and tank top hidden under a sweatshirt wouldn't work tonight. The temperature wasn't likely to drop below 85 degrees all night. Bad enough that next to Isa Sam looked dumpier than ever, she didn't want to be sweating like a hog, too.

In the back of her mind, she heard Isa nagging her "You need to stop being so negative. You're beautiful! You've got dangerous curves." But that was just how Isa was and Sam didn't buy it for a second.

By the time she was dressed there was no doubt she was going to be a bit late. She'd finally settled on a sundress she'd bought once in a fit of optimism but had never worn before. It was long and flowing, strapless, and had a pretty floral pattern in pinks and soft greens.

Sam felt weird being in colors other than black and denim, but if she pulled the top up as high as possible it wasn't that bad. At any rate she wouldn't pass out from heatstroke and regain consciousness only to die of embarrassment.

Late though she was, she still beat Isa.

Aiden was waiting alone by the gates to the fairground, lounging against the chain link fence with one hand stuck in his pocket and looking like a Greek god.

If the gods wore flip flops, shorts, and white tee shirts.

Sam almost turned and fled at the idea of being alone with him. If she had to make small talk with last night's amazing dream running through her head -and it was- who knew what she might blurt out?

But it was too late, Aiden saw her and waved, then jogged up to meet her. When he got close he stopped and took her in from her shaggy curls to her leather sandals, taking his time with all the things in between.

Sam was suddenly aware that the neckline of her dress had been creeping south, exposing a fair amount of cleavage, and the wind was blowing her skirt tight against her legs. He gave a low whistle. "Miss, sorry I mean Sam, you are looking beautiful this evening."

"Um, thanks..." Sam tugged at her dress. Stupid thing. Stupid boobs, why you gotta be so big? She fumbled for something to say that wouldn't be absolutely embarrassing or inane. "Um. Sorry I'm late. How long have you been waiting?"

"Not long, don't worry," he smiled. "It's nice to see you again."

Great, and I'm going to spend the whole evening blushing it would seem. I hope the sun sets fast so nobody can tell. "I'll text Isa and see where she is."

"You don't need to bother, she texted me a few minutes ago. She'll be along soon."

"Oh." Idiot. Of course they'd be texting each other. She's the girlfriend, or the soon-to-be girlfriend anyway.

"Do you like roller coasters?" he asked.

Sam shook her head, "Not really. They remind me of things like gravity, and grievous bodily harm, and my own mortality."

She was fiercely proud to see that Isa wasn't the only one who could make him laugh. He had a nice laugh, not a bray or a snigger. "Good. You can be my excuse. Isabella says she wants to go on all of them. Twice. And while I am a manly man who knows no fear, I am quite relieved to offer my services as an earthbound companion."

"We can play games," Sam ventured, "And pet the world's tiniest horse."

"It's a date," Aiden quickly replied.

Aaand I'm blushing again thought Sam.

Then she spied Isa strolling through the crowd towards them. She was sorry to have their one on one time ended so soon, and pleased to realize that if Aiden had been telling the truth about roller coasters then there would be much more one on one time to come. And she felt guilty for feeling so possessive of the man who was technically Isa's date.

Chapter 7 -- Haunted house

Once inside, Aiden suggested they walk the perimeter of the fair first, to get their bearings and plan their evening. He also strongly recommended that they select a spot to meet up should they get separated. "What?" he asked when he caught Sam and Isa both trying not to laugh.

Isa lost the battle and guffawed, so Sam explained. "That was 100% cop. A plan of attack? And we all have cell phones." Of course, you don't have my number. She grinned at the thought of being that bold, but couldn't actually force the words out.

They agreed that in case of separation, emergency, or extreme thirst they should meet up at the beer tent. And just to be sure they knew the way, they found it on the grounds map and meandered over.

Sam bought her friends each a beer and herself a glass of wine. As she nursed it she watched the other two chat. They were trying to figure out the most efficient way to see the whole fair, a process hampered by the necessity of swinging by each roller coaster multiple times. Isa was adamant on that point.

They're not acting as lovey-dovey as I'd have thought. I don't get it, but I like it.

After their drinks they wasted some money on games. "We got in free," Isa explained, "It's only honorable to let ourselves get robbed now that we're here." So they dutifully lost money at the ring toss, and the dime toss, and the goldfish game.

But at the air rifle range Aiden won a prize. He selected a stuffed shark with a lopsided grin and eyes that bugged out. He presented it to Isa with a little bow and a barely audible "Thank you."

Sam immediately looked away, pretending to scan the midway for the next thing to do. If they were going to get cute, they should have some privacy and anyway she didn't want to look.

Just a few minutes later, Isa handed her shark back to Aiden and her purse to Sam, so she wouldn't drop them while she got her first roller coaster fix. Across from it was a haunted house, and Aiden took Sam's hand and pulled her into the line.

Sam felt ridiculous in her uncomfortably girly dress in a line full of couples. Rebelliously she decided that there was no harm in pretending that they were just another couple for a little while. No harm to anyone but me anyway, and I'm going to wind up alone at the end of the night either way.

So as they entered the haunted house and a blast of air startled her, she didn't fight her impulse to shriek and inch closer to Aiden. He is a big, safe, cop after all. No double motives here.

He threw an arm around her shoulders and pulled her in close to him. She breathed deep to catch his smell; coconut shampoo, and under it the smell of his body which was subtle but utterly masculine.

A giant animatronic spider popped out of the wall with a metallic hiss and Sam flinched. Keep those spiders coming she thought, and wrapped her arms tight around Aiden's waist.

Isa was waiting when they emerged, looking beautiful and happy and, most of all, quite windblown. Sam self-consciously released her grip on Aiden, but he let his arm remain casually draped across her shoulders.

They rode the merry go round next. Isa insisted because she knew Sam loved it but wouldn't speak up about it on her own, too embarrassed to ask to go on a kid's ride. This wasn't any shoddy little merry go round, however. It was a classic one, made by the Wurlitzer Company more than 100 years ago, with two tiers and real horsehair in the tails of some of the bigger horses. It had always seemed magical to Sam.

They selected a row of three horses in the top tier. The horses were smaller on this level, but the view of the fair was lovely.

Before the ride began, Isa insisted on taking a picture. So they crammed together as close as possible around the center horse. Aiden hugged them both close, one on either side while Isa held her phone out at arm's length to capture all three of them. Then the ride operator yelled to get on their horses properly and stop fooling around, did they think he had all night? Sam was mortified, but Isa and Aiden laughed their heads off as the ride began.

Chapter 8 -- Freak show

"This looks like my grandma," Aiden mused, looking at a framed newspaper photograph of the Fiji Mermaid. Then, abashed, "Not that she isn't a very nice lady. She's very active in her church."

Sam grinned. Her mental image was of a human sized fish-monkey with Aiden's curls gone gray, busily trying to organize a bake sale while the congregation dropped loose change into an offering plate to buy the right to watch. It wasn't the kind of idea that can easily be packed into a one-liner however, so she let it pass.

They were meandering around one of the many disappointing freak tents while Isa rode a roller coaster yet again. There were only three adult coasters in the whole midway, but Isa had ridden them each at least four times and didn't show signs of stopping.

In the meanwhile Sam was learning quite a bit about Aiden: He was a gentleman, not in the show-offy kind of way but the awkward way of a genuinely good person in a generally rude world. He liked fried onions and diet cola. When he listened to her talk, it felt like she was the most important person in the world. And he was absolutely terrified of horses, even very tiny ones.

They'd moved on to the boredom of the freak show tent to let Aiden calm down from his pony induced trauma, and so far he still hadn't let go of Sam's hand.

One of the greatest tragedies of the modern era, Sam mused, is that a room full of newspaper clippings and paper mache models is what's considered a freak show.

She felt like she was on a roller coaster ride herself. When they were alone it felt almost as if Aiden liked her. It felt like a date. And then Isa would turn up again and suddenly Sam wasn't sure. Aiden and Isa weren't acting like they were anything special, but this had been their idea to start with. Sam was the tag-along, wasn't she? She wasn't sure any more and it was driving her nuts.

She screwed up her courage. "Aiden, what's-" but when he turned to look at her she froze up. "What's up with this guy?" she pointed at another ancient clipping. Sam, you coward.

Aiden peered at the clipping, then shrugged, "I have no idea."

"So... not another of your relatives, then?"

He laughed. But when he was finished laughing he didn't look away from her. He gazed at her face with a hint of a smile still on his lips. For her part, Sam could not take her eyes off those lips. They were elegant and expressive, and they looked soft. He had just a little bit of beard stubble on his chin, and its ruggedness contrasted enticingly with his sculpted mouth. Sam imagined feeling those lips on hers. She wondered how they would taste, and how they would feel playing up and down her skin.

On impulse she stepped forward. This close she had to tilt her face up to look at him. He grasped her bare shoulders, stroked her skin. Is this really happening? She parted her lips, not sure what to say but feeling like something had to happen.

What happened was that Aiden covered her mouth with his. He was gentle, his lips brushing hers delicately. The bristles on his chin just barely touched her skin. Sam wrapped her fingers around the back of his neck and pulled his head down, returning the kiss hungrily.

He tasted sweet. She wanted this so badly, and after two days of uncertainty all she knew was that she had him right now. She wanted all the now she could get.

Her mouth surrendered to his questing tongue, her heart was racing and she felt weak. He wrapped an arm around the small of her back and she knew that she would not fall. She kept her eyes firmly shut. If I open them, I might wake up. She pressed against him firmly, inviting more, using her lips and tongue to beg him to pleasure her. He placed his free hand on her side, his fingers curled around her ribcage, his thumb teasing her nipple under the thin sundress. She moaned and he pulled back to look at her. She couldn't stifle her sigh as their mouths parted.

Reluctantly, she opened her eyes. He didn't disappear or turn into an alarm clock. His lips were red and his hair was mussed up. His pupils were huge in his blue eyes.

Those eyes held a question, but he didn't seem to know what it was. "Sam?" was all he managed, his voice hoarse.

"Shut up," she panted, and that was good enough for him. She melted against his body as his mouth scorched hers. She nipped his bottom lip with her teeth. He backed her against a plexiglass case and ran his hands up and down her, feeling her body under the flowing cotton.

The way he looked at her and touched her, she knew he found her sexy. The realization made her bold, and she let her own hands explore his body.

First his arms and chest, then his butt and thighs. His gasping breaths told her he liked her touch. His hands were on her chest now, and she arched her back, pressing into his palms.

Suddenly there was a stern "Ahem!" from the front of the tent. Sam and Aiden jumped and tried to act like they had just been inspecting the contents of the Plexiglas display case, which turned out to be a taxidermied two headed calf. The carny was not fooled. "I don't care what you do in here," he growled, "Until you start to damage the artifacts. You all can get out now."

Red faced and with clothing slightly askew, Sam and Aiden slunk out. "And I don't want to see you in my tent again!" the man's words followed them. As they adjusted their clothing Sam sighed inwardly, well it was nice while it lasted. But even as she resigned herself, Aiden caught her hand and spun her to look at him. He scooped her up in his arms and planted a soft kiss on her lips.

"You're amazing," he whispered in her ear. He placed her back on the ground but put his arm possessively around her waist.

Flummoxed, Sam said "Shut up." But she said it softly and cuddled closer. A sudden vibration in Aiden's pocket startled her. At the same time her own phone gave a little beep. They both had a text. It was from Isa and it said TOO MUCH BEER AND COASTERS. VERY SICK. LITTLE HELP?

Chapter 9 -- First time

It took them ten frantic minutes to find her sitting on a bench near the end of the midway, looking very pale. She smiled weakly. "Good time, but I think I'm ready to go now." Her eyes lingered on their clasped hands for a second, she narrowed her eyes, and then she threw up again.

"I can't believe we just let her drink and go on rides all evening. We have to get her to bed. Isa hon, where's your car?"

"I took the bus. Thought I might have a few drinks."

A few? Well, that makes it easier anyway. "Aiden can you drive us to her house? I'll put her to bed quick, then you can drop me at my place. I'll come back for my car in the morning."

He seemed a bit surprised to have her usurp his role as protector and authority figure, but accepted his role as chauffer with good grace. "Of course. I'll go get my car and meet you at the side gate. It's closer. You two can come along at her pace." Sam looked at him gratefully and he sprinted off.

Sam was glad that Isa wasn't in any condition to talk. She knew she would have to explain what had happened between her and Aiden, but she didn't know how her friend would react. She had seemed pretty ticked off, right before the puking. Puking would make me ticked off, though.

On one hand, this evening had been a plan between Aiden and Isa, Sam was the third wheel. But on the other, Aiden's behavior showed such a strong preference for Sam that even she couldn't doubt it. She would be glad to have time to sort out her feelings.

The drive to Isa's place was quick and quiet. Sam left Aiden in the car, promising to be quick, though he pressed her to take as much time as necessary to make sure Isa was going to be fine. Sam urged Isa to drink some water, then helped her change into pajamas. Hmmm... she couldn't help but notice that Isa was wearing a plain bra and cotton panties, not granny panties, but not what I would imagine Isa would pick if she were trying to hook up. Feeling somewhat relieved, she tucked Isa into bed.

"Ok, just pay attention for a sec and then you can sleep, ok?" Isa blearily tried to focus on her face. "Your phone is right here by the bed. Call me if you need anything or start to get sick again, promise?"

Isa nodded. She was already falling asleep and Sam was pretty sure she'd be fine. She hadn't been drunk as much as dehydrated and dizzy.

She told Aiden as much as she climbed into his car. He looked relieved, but not relieved like he'd been terribly worried. Friendly relieved, not love relieved. And yet, for the moment the magic between them seemed broken.

They rode to Sam's apartment in silence, and he walked her to her door. I can't just say nothing. Sam Morgan, don't you dare let this guy walk away without saying anything!

Maybe the events of the evening had exhausted her shyness, because she was able to meet Aiden's eyes and say, "Thank you. I really enjoyed what we - I mean, I had an amazing time tonight." In her mind she could picture his face as he'd called her amazing.

His answer was simple and direct: he kissed her. It was a gentle, lingering kiss but she could feel him tremble slightly. It lasted a short infinity, and when he broke contact

Sam had made up her mind. "Do you want to come in?"

They crashed through the door and Sam just barely had the presence of mind to shut it behind them before he picked her up by the waist and literally tossed her onto the bed.

She laughed in surprise but he cut her off with a kiss. This kiss was neither slow, nor gentle; it made her toes curl and kindled a fire in her. By the time he released her mouth she was practically frantic with desire. She pulled his tee off over his head so she could see his gorgeous chest. He had a claddagh tattoo over his heart, a detail that had not been in her dream. She ran her hands across his abs, kissing his skin. Experimentally, she grazed her tongue over his nipple and he gasped.

He slipped a hand under her skirt and rubbed her inner thigh, and when she moaned against his chest he caressed her mound, teasing the cleft beneath the fabric of her panties with his fingertips. Her body responded with a will of its own, her hips lifted up, trying to increase the pressure of his hand, and she raked her fingernails down his back as she whimpered.

With a smooth motion, he lifted her just enough to slip her dress off her and paused to admire her as she lay before him. The lust on his face was plain to read. She sat up, trying to capture his mouth in hers again, but he caressed her again through her panties and she sank back to the mattress.

Aiden hooked a finger into her underwear and slipped them off her. Then he unclasped her bra and she was completely bare. Dimly she was aware of just how shameless she must seem, wriggling naked on the bed, but she was so hungry for him she couldn't help herself. At that moment she would have done anything at all that he wanted, and there was pleasure in the surrender.

He traced his lips across her belly, and took her nipple in his mouth. "Aaaahh..." she purred. His mouth was hot and wet. His tongue rasped against the sensitive tissue, and when he sucked gently there was an aching sort of bliss that she had never felt before.

Aiden unzipped his shorts and slid them off. He guided her legs apart and mounted her, entering her with a smooth, forceful thrust.

Sam gasped. In her dream he hadn't felt so huge! He saw the look in her eyes and kissed her. With one hand he reached between her legs and found her clit with his fingertips. He teased her, circling it, then gently stroking and she relaxed around him as she focused on the intense sensations he could cause with such delicate movements.

He began to thrust, sliding in and out of her wet folds and she joined in the rhythm, bringing her hips up to meet his. The way they moved in time, the way she couldn't tell where his pleasure ended and hers began, made it feel to Sam like they were one thing. Like they'd always been meant to join like this.

Feelings and sensations rose to a breaking point inside Sam. The climax was almost unbearably intense. She cried out and clung to Aiden as wave after wave of release shook her. He clutched her tight and thrust a final time, letting her body push him over the edge with her. Sam heard him shout her name through the blood rushing in her ears.

For a while they lay together, not speaking. Caressing and kissing idly as they caught their breath and regained their senses.

Wow, Sam thought, wow.

Then, since she couldn't think of a reason not to, she said it out loud. "Aiden, wow."

"Wow." He agreed. "Have I mentioned you're amazing?"

"Not recently enough," she teased, kissing his cheek.

"You're amazing. Can we -- ?" He was cut off by his phone ringing in his pants pocket on the floor. He groaned and reached over her bare body to retrieve it, glanced at it and exploded up off the bed. "Shit shit shit shit!" He fumbled to pull on his pants, and jerked his shirt back on. "I've got to go NOW." He gave her a dry peck on the cheek and then he was gone, leaving an insufficient "Sorry!" in his wake.

Chapter 10 -- A swift retreat

What the actual hell?

Sam was left alone and confused. Since she was already naked she got in the shower, hoping the hot water would wash away some of her doubt and keep away the hurt she could feel building.

A girl only had one first time. She really had not expected hers to end with her lover literally running away at top speed. Had this all been some sort of trick? Con the virgin into giving it up for you, it'll be easy because she's so desperate!

She punched the shower wall weakly as tears started to fall. She didn't really know much about how romance was supposed to work, but she knew it wasn't supposed to be like this.

She tried to think it through logically and got nowhere. Aiden had seemed genuinely interested, but objectively none of his behavior made any sense. If Sam was his goal, why make plans with Isa? Why not just ask for Sam's number. Why run out just now? Maybe I was right from the start. Maybe he's just a numb nuts jerk.

That night she dreamed she was lost in a big, dark room. She couldn't see where she was going and the only sound was mocking laughter drifting to her ears from a great distance.

Saturday morning she woke up feeling a little sore. She was nursing her second coffee when Uncle Ty called. "Hey kiddo, still want to get out of town?"

"So bad. You got things worked out I take it?"

"Yes. I'm emailing you the hotel information, the files you'll need and the meeting time. I've got two flights available. Do you want to leave at nine, or at noon?"

Sam glanced at the clock. 8:45. Is he being funny or does he genuinely not know how time works? "Better make it noon. I need to do some stuff." Like pick up my car and try to scrub off the stink of remorse.

"All right. That's set. Try not to call me while you're there unless it's an emergency. My hands are going to be tied..." His tone conveyed the image of a suggestively raised eyebrow.

"Didn't need to know that. Will do."

"Have a good weekend, kid."

"You too, Uncle Ty." He laughed devilishly and the call ended. Sam pounded the last of her coffee. She had two hours to get her stuff together and get to the airport. In some places you could afford to ignore the 'arrive one hour prior to your flight' advisement, but not at Buffalo International Airport. The security lines were like the world's slowest game of Russian roulette.

She threw some clothes in a bag, and considered her swimsuit but it was looking pretty sad. Screw it, I'll buy a nice new one while I'm there. Even if I have to tear Virginia Beach apart to find one that looks good on me.

She cleaned the cat litter and set up the usual weekend travel arrangement: Extra food, extra water plus an open toilet lid, and a call to her neighbor to check in on Deadpool once or twice. She called a cab to come take her to her own car, and was showered and dressed by the time it arrived.

She left her car in weekend parking at precisely 10:45 and gave herself a pat on the back. As she was queueing up for the security check, her phone beeped. Isa had texted her the picture from the merry go round. Ugh. I did not need to see this right now. Isa looked like a fairy princess and Aiden looked like her white knight. Sam looked like a dumb, dumpy girl who had no idea what was in store.

The line was not moving, and Sam estimated she had at least 40 minutes of waiting left, so she called her friend. "Hey you. How're you feeling?"

"So much better. Thanks for taking care of my pathetic butt."

Sam decided she was ready to start getting some answers. "No problem. Uh, listen Isa, you're not mad at me or anything right?"

"No. What? I have no idea what you're talking about."

"I kind of - I don't even know what to call it - I guess 'took over' Aiden last night." She tapped her foot, waiting for Isa to stop laughing and be able to speak again.

"You idiot. That was the whole plan!" She cracked up again. "You mean he didn't tell you? I figured he must've pretty early on because you two got real close real fast."

When Sam failed to respond, Isa explained that when she'd left the office after Aiden the day before yesterday, it was because she had a hunch that he was interested in Sam. "But he's as awkward as you are. He was about to give up on you so I hatched a cunning and devious plan to get you two crazy kids together. But he was supposed to fill you in on it. The dork."

Sam tried to wrap her head around this. She was relieved to know Isa wasn't angry or hurt, but she still was. What Isa was saying didn't jive with her memory of Aiden's sudden retreat. *Why would he not explain the date setup to me? Is he so afraid of commitment that even a real date would be too much?*

"So how'd it go once you put me to bed? Did Aiden put you to bed?" I think I need to stop letting Isa spend so much time with Uncle Ty. I can't tell who's worse. But she was glad to have her friend to talk to. She explained to Isa everything that had happened, from the kiss to Aiden's abrupt departure. When she was finished, Isa was nonplussed.

"Face it, Isa. He used us."

"I don't buy it. The kid's not bright enough."

"Whatever. I'm over it."

"Yeah, you really sound over it. And he hasn't texted you or called to explain?"

"He doesn't have my number."

"Oh! You'd think he'd have thought to get it from me, but oh well. I'll just get in touch with him and tell him to call you."

"Oh god. Please don't. I'm about to get on a plane, but even if I wasn't I don't want to talk to the jerk."

"You just have a hard time believing anyone likes you. You have to get over that."

I got over it last night and look where that got me. "Just leave it alone, OK Isa? I'm calling a mulligan on the whole thing. It never happened and I'm still a virgin and I'm going to Virginia Beach, an entire beach dedicated to my virgin status."

"Oh sweetie. I wish I could give you a hug. Just don't work yourself up into a huff, ok? I think going and having a fun weekend is the right idea."

"Yeah. Listen, I've got to go through the scanner now," Sam lied, "I'll call you in a day or two, ok?"

"Sure, hon. Bye."

"Bye."

Sam tried to follow her friend's advice with limited success for the entirety of the long, frustrating process of boarding the plane.

Chapter 11 -- Confrontation

She took care of the meeting with Mr. Kodama Saturday evening, shortly after her arrival at the hotel. Uncle Ty had given her a long weekend, so she had all of Sunday and most of Monday to enjoy herself and she devoted herself to that goal with more zeal than normal.

She hadn't had to tear the town apart to find a swimsuit. Instead she had gone to an upscale establishment and treated herself to an expensive one piece. Worth it, though. She hadn't felt this good in a swimsuit since she was a little kid. It was blue with little white flowers all over it. It looked more like a vintage corset than anything else and Sam adored it.

She was lying on her towel, reading a cheap thriller and drying herself in the sun after a swim. Occasionally a male passerby would give her an appreciative glance, which made Sam a little self-conscious, but mostly the attention was a much needed balm to her bruised ego.

Maybe I should pick someone up. If someone uses you, use someone else, that's how it works, right? One man, maybe 30 years old and looking very good in his green Hawaiian print trunks, had given her a look that was an open invitation as he'd walked past. He was enjoying a margarita under an umbrella a little ways down the beach.

Sam imagined walking up to him like she was some sort of sex goddess, and just picking him up right now. I could do that thing women do in movies where they drink from a straw but somehow imply that the straw is the guy's penis.

Or maybe she would just lean in close, stroke him through his trunks, whisper her room number in his ear and walk away. She'd be in the hot tub with nothing on when he got to her room. He'll do me against the wall, Sam decided, hard enough that the next room will complain about the noise. And it won't hurt when he disappears because I'll be the one to disappear.

She sighed. It was tempting but she wasn't really that girl. I'd embarrass myself trying to be sexy like that.

It was nice to think about, though.

She decided to go to her room alone and think about it some more. She figured if she kept her mind full of enough random strangers it might eventually stop drifting back to Aiden.

She couldn't get the jerk out of her head for long. Even now, as she walked up the beach towards her hotel she couldn't shake the image of him. She even thought she could see him, that guy picking his way across the sand, looked just like him.

It was the third time she'd thought she'd seen him in the crowd. The first time it had happened, her heart had leapt with joy. It had all been a misunderstanding! He had cared so much he couldn't even wait for her return to explain. But she'd come to her senses afterward. If she saw him again he would just hurt her again. Every time she'd seen him he'd insulted her, or made her feel awkward, or hurt her.

The guy was coming closer. Close enough for Sam to realize that his features were not going to rearrange themselves into those of a stranger. That's either him or his eviller twin. Somehow, against all logic, he was here. Sam did the only thing that made sense to her: She turned and fled.

She was barefoot and his legs were long. Even with her head start he reached her on the steps to the hotel, catching her wrist in his hand and spinning her to face him. She jerked out of his grip and glared at him, panting.

"Sam! Please let me explain. If I'd known it was your first time I would have made it special, but - ", wham, Sam slapped him, hard, across the face.

"It was special to me, asshole! But apparently not to you. THAT'S why I'm pissed." She glared at him.

A few bystanders were drawing close, curious about the scuffle. One called out, "Hey lady, want us to call the cops?"

"Maybe hotel security. This jerk is a cop."

"Figures," the stranger laughed. He didn't go anywhere.

"Sam," Aiden stepped closer to her and lowered his voice, trying to not be overheard by the conspicuous eavesdroppers.

"Just listen. I had to go fast and I was pretty scared. My partner had to respond to a scene alone because I missed his call."

He spread his hands and dropped his eyes. "I missed the call because I was so busy with you." He winced at his own phrasing. "I mean, I was so focused on you, and...us. It was special to me."

Sam said nothing.

He plunged on, "And I should have explained about the date to you. I thought it was wrong to mislead you but Isabella's very persuasive. And then I was so distracted by that dress I just forgot."

He searched her face, trying to gauge her reaction. She tried hard to keep it blank, determined not to be so easily swayed this time. "And I should have just asked for your number to start with. And I should have apologized for being unprofessional the night we met. And I should have been more professional the night we met. I'm sorry, Sam. I get stupid around you. I can't help it, you go to my head."

There was a circle of curious beachgoers around them now. "C'mon, honey," an older woman in an enormous hat hollered, "That's the kind of apology you don't get from just any man!" She gave the portly man at her side a meaningful look.

Sam didn't know if she wanted to laugh or cry, but she knew she didn't want to do it in front of so many witnesses. "C'mon," she mumbled, and stalked towards the hotel doors, pushing through the dispersing crowd. Aiden obeyed immediately, his face a portrait of hope.

Chapter 12 -- Finally, a hot shower

Sam pressed a hand to her forehead as she made a beeline through the lobby of her hotel towards the elevators, acutely aware of Aiden trailing behind her. Like a puppy.

A little grin cracked her stony expression. Argh! I was ready to murder him five minutes ago. Didn't my life used to be boring? I distinctly remember being boring last week.

She'd forgiven him a fraction of a second after her palm made contact with his face, but her body was a bit slow to catch up; adrenaline was still coursing through her, and her heart was racing. What I need to do is burn off all this energy. And then her earlier fantasies came back to mind and she thought why the hell not?

As the elevator doors slid closed behind them, Sam hit the STOP button and rounded on Aiden. She didn't know how long it would last, but right now she felt like a wild animal and she intended to use that, hopefully to the advantage of both of them. Putting both palms on Aiden's chest she shoved him against the elevator wall. It only worked because he was so surprised, but it gave her a rush of satisfaction to hear him thump against the polished steel.

"So you're sorry, hmmm?" she growled.

His eyes widened. Apparently this was not what he'd expected. Good. "I am so sorry I hurt you."

"Good." She pulled his face down to hers and kissed him. She felt his teeth against hers, and explored his mouth with her tongue almost viciously. God he tastes good.

"Because you're going to pay me back. Right now."

She pressed her body full up against him, acutely aware that she was still wearing only a swimsuit. She cupped him in her hand, just as she had pictured doing to the stranger on the beach. She knew now that the reason she hadn't acted on that impulse was that it simply wouldn't have been right. What she wanted was Aiden.

When he was semi-hard and panting she released him, re-activated the elevator and selected her floor. Luckily, no one else entered until they reached her floor, because they would have walked in on Aiden kissing her neck and trailing his lips across her bosom, massaging her breasts, and murmuring her name as he ground against her body.

When the doors opened they dashed down the hall to her room. Inside, Aiden tried to lead her to the bed but she raised a finger.

"Who's in charge here?" she teased, but softened her words with another intimate caress.

Her suite was not the most expensive in the hotel, but it was quit luxurious. Among other amenities it featured a lavish bathroom equipped with an enormous shower that had not one but six showerheads, one on each short end and two on each of the walls. This was where she directed him to go. After a second he caught on and turned the water on, adjusting the temperature until it was delightfully steamy.

She slipped off her swimsuit while his back was turned. She fully intended to keep him surprised. When he turned around and saw her, posed coquettishly with her hands behind her back, one leg bent, back arched and chest high, he stared. As Sam watched, the flabbergasted expression left his face, replaced by purpose and passion.

He advanced slowly, taking control of the situation with every step. Sam watched him avidly, he moves like a panther, she thought. She backed away, to make the moment last, but in only two steps her back hit the chilly tile wall and Aiden closed the gap between them.

His hands seemed to be everywhere at once; her buttocks, her breasts, her thighs and belly, and especially her sex. Everywhere he touched her nerves came alive, blazing with sensation.

He dropped to his knees before her and buried his mouth in her cleft. She twined her fingers in his hair, needing something to hold on to and inadvertently drew him harder into her.

She groaned as his tongue flicked and swirled around, feeling herself grow hot and moist. With every caress of his lips and tongue, her knees got weaker. She felt him slip two fingers up into her, stroking inside in time to the motions of his mouth. Her pleasure overcame her in a glorious moment, her hips rocked as she threw her head back and her body convulsed.

Aiden stood up before her, and without him to lean on she sank to the floor. He undressed slowly for her, letting her take in the sight of his muscular arms and chest, turning to flaunt his tight butt as he dropped his shorts and then facing her again. He was fully erect, and she could not keep her eyes from his manhood as he took his turn posing for her.

On impulse she crawled forward and took him into her mouth. She tasted a salty droplet on the head of his shaft as she licked and sucked. He was trembling on the brink when, gasping, he pushed her back.

He picked her up and she wrapped her legs around his waist. He carried her into the shower and braced her against the wall, under a stream of warm water. There, with her legs still encircling him he plunged into her until she enveloped him entirely.

Sam clutched him and whispered, "Oh god yes!" as he pumped his hips, plunging into her. The feeling of him slipping in and out of her was exquisite, and she pushed back as hard as she could, driving him into her.

His movements were coming faster and faster and his breath was ragged. Sam felt the tension and heat in her loins blazing and she begged him, "Don't stop! Oh, please don't stop!" He slammed into her and she exploded in his arms. She jerked and screamed his name, her body shuddered and rapture flooded her. At the same time, Aiden cried out in blissful agony, shuddering and spilling his seed into her.

First Love

They collapsed onto the shower floor in a tangled heap. It was a long time before either felt ready to stand up.

Chapter 13 -- Going for the jugular

A week later Sam, Aiden and Isa were sharing Thai food on Sam's lunch break. Uncle Ty had been gone for half the morning because his new lady, Ramona, worked nights and had an odd schedule. He had promised to be back an hour ago.

"So you guys are a thing now, right? No more drama?" Isa asked around a mouthful of noodles. She fixed a steely gaze on Aiden. "You have at least got her number?"

Aiden pretended not to hear, and Sam laughed. "Yes, he has my number. And we're going on an actual, real, normal-person date tomorrow. We're going to the museum."

Isa rolled her eyes. "You need a new definition of normal." She munched for a minute and then seemed to reconsider. "Well, whatever makes you happy."

Sam grinned at her friend. She was happy. She was learning to trust that Aiden wasn't going to disappear or abandon her, and if he wasn't really learning to remember to tell her important things, she was getting better at asking. It was working out. She was wanted, and she basked in that feeling.

Uncle Ty walked in and called a distracted hello to Sam and Isa as he walked to his desk. Then he stopped and backed up. Leaning past Isa and across Sam's desk he looked Aiden in the eye and growled, "And just who the hell are you?" His tone implied that the younger man would have been beneath his notice were he not so disgusting, like a slug or a maggot.

Aiden stood nervously and proffered a hand. "Aiden Williams, sir. I'm Sam's, uh... that is I'm dating your..." he gulped.

"We were thinking of breaking in my desk this weekend, actually." Sam interrupted.

Isa choked on her noodles, and Aiden just choked. Uncle Tyrone went white and his hands clenched at his sides. Sam could see Uncle Ty processing the mental image, maybe imagining Aiden doing to her what Ty did to his chain of female admirers. Aiden backed away and it was a good thing he did because Uncle Ty scooped up a letter opener and, leaping over Sam's desk, went for the jugular.

Later he claimed it was all in good fun but Aiden never visited Sam at work again. Nevertheless, they made each other quite happy for quite some time.

THE END

Keep reading for a

Sneak Preview of

"REBOUND LOVE",

Book 2

in the

Samantha's

LOVE & ROMANCE

Series.

Denise Daniella Darcy

Sneak Preview of REBOUND LOVE, Book 2

Chapter 1 -- Erotic yoga

"Now really reach into that stretch," the instructor bubbled at the front of the room. "Keep your center. Good!"

Sam felt ridiculous. She was in a room with a dozen elastic-clad women. Every one of them was on their own little plastic rug with her bottom stuck up into the air. *Is my center the place that didn't want to notice that everyone here is thinner than me? Because I think I found it.*

It wasn't that Sam was fat, there was just too much of her. She had wide hips and a round rear end and her breasts were always in the way. Even her brown hair was big. Its thick brown curls were currently falling into her eyes.

The instructor called out a new position, and Sam had no idea what it was. Every position had a ridiculous and supposedly mystical name, like Irritated Crab and Crane Shrugging. *When do we do Woman Getting Out of Here?* Isa had convinced her that tagging along to her yoga class would be good for her.

"You never do anything, you need to get out of the house. And work doesn't count."

"I don't want to get out of the house. The house is where my cat and pajamas and the internet all are. I've never been a joiner and it never bugged you before." She and Isa had already had variations on this conversation at least a billion times and she had known where it was going. She hated where it was going.

"It's not good for you now that Aiden's gone." Isa had put on her mom voice. Sam groaned. "If you just stew alone you'll never move on." And eventually, Sam had grudgingly agreed to come accompany Isa today.

She scrambled to copy what the incredibly flexible stranger in front of her was doing. She tried not to give Isa a dirty look, as her friend stretched and contorted lithely at her side. Normally Sam didn't mind that Isa was everything she wanted to be: Outgoing, thin, athletic, and blonde. Today it pricked at her insecurities and made her more irritated.

Maybe I don't want to get over him. She arched her back in an approximation of the proper motion. The last time she and Aiden had been together, he'd bent her backwards and kissed her all over, from her navel to her throat. She remembered how his fingertips had traced up and down her spine. The feeling was delicious and it made her shiver. His tanned hands stood out against her ivory skin as he massaged and teased her. He knew all her most sensitive secret places. He kissed her nipples, and they crinkled under his soft, smooth lips. He nibbled the lobes of her ears, his breath soft and his cheek pressed to her cheek. Then he had kissed her deep and with passion. When he released her mouth her lips had been throbbing and she felt a flush in her cheeks.

Remembering, Sam's body relaxed and she threw herself into the stretch. She imagined Aiden's hungry hands and mouth and shut her eyes. "Mmmmm..." she breathed.

When he rolled over and placed her on top of him she'd straddled him and eased herself onto his shaft. With her flesh enveloping his and her arms behind her head she rode him. Her hips rocked slowly at first, gently provoking moans from his lips, and stoking the pulsing heat inside her. As her pleasure grew, she pushed harder, and he met her thrust for thrust. As they moved together she could feel him slipping in and out of her slick tightness. He reached up and stroked her, then pinched her sensitive nipple in his fingers. She gasped and her rhythm increased, the needy edge of her passion coming to the forefront. She ground him into her, and he pounded back. "Oh, god, Aiden," she whispered on shallow breath, "I'm coming!"

Her pleasure shot through her with blistering intensity. Her muscles contracted around him sending another wave of sensation through her. She was still feeling little waves and tremors as Aiden flipped her over and topped her. Sensitive as she was now, his swift thrusts drove her back over the edge. She bit her lip and her breath came in ragged gasps as she exploded again. Aiden groaned and came with her, his body shaking with the violence of the pleasure he took from her. They'd fallen asleep later, still naked, with their legs tangled together, clinging to each other like survivors of a shipwreck embrace a life ring.

As the memory faded, Sam realized that the class had gone entirely silent. She opened her eyes to see every eye in the room on her. The instructor had gone pale and her mouth was wide open. To her horror, she wasn't even doing one of the yoga stretches anymore. No, she was flat on her back, knees bent, legs open. *Oh my god. What was I doing?* She thought hard and realized she had been speaking out loud. *I said I was coming. I was moaning. Oh no! Please tell me I wasn't humping thin air.* She groaned.

Beside Sam, Isa had her hands over her mouth trying to hold in her laughter even as her eyes tried to convey sympathy and concern. The other students looked baffled for a moment. Then, rippling from one end of the room to the other the giggles started.

The instructor coughed and managed to squeak, "I think class is over for today. Good, uuuh, good job everyone."

Sam had to withstand the looks and whispers of all the cute little yoga girls in the locker room as she threw her jeans and sweatshirt back on. Isa, who was the type of person who wore yoga pants everywhere just because, was waiting for her at the front doors. When they got into Isa's car, she threw her arms around Sam. "Girlfriend, we have got to get that imagination of yours under control."

Sam squeezed her eyes shut and stared at the ceiling of the Hyundai. "How bad was it?"

Isa squeezed her hand. "It was pretty bad. You don't want the gory details. You want to watch enough reality TV to cause brain damage so you can forget this ever happened."

Sam gave her friend a sick grin. "Forget what ever happened?"

"That's the spirit!"

But I'm much better at dwelling and obsessing than forgetting, Sam thought, as she tried to shower off her feelings. Intense, lingering embarrassment mingled with the depression and regret she'd been carrying already. She cried a little, in the tired way of someone who has cried much more than they ought to already.

Aiden had had to go back to his hometown on the West Coast, almost exactly as far from Buffalo and Sam as possible without leaving the country. She couldn't blame him, his mother was very ill and needed constant care from someone responsible. Aiden's overprotective streak had developed as a reaction to the deadbeat nature of the rest of his family, so the woman had nobody else to turn to.

It's still completely unfair, though.

Sam couldn't leave her job. Uncle Ty relied on her, but more than that her work was important to her self-respect. She didn't have much to be proud of except how she'd built herself up from a humble coffee girl to junior partner. The thought of not being that any more terrified her to the core.

Neither of them had been worried about the distance, at first.

Sam had blithely assumed that the difficulties of a long distance relationship would be nothing compared to the power and brilliance of their love. *God, I was so wrong.* Even though Sam could afford to fly out to see him nearly once a week their relationship had crumbled before her eyes.

She couldn't understand the pressure he was under as the full time caregiver to a proud woman. From across the continent she couldn't even lend a helping hand. As she felt him pull away from her, her faith in him had shattered. He could see it happening but was powerless to reassure her.

He didn't deserve her insecurity and doubt, she knew, and her guilt only made her defensive. *We were such a mess.*

The end had come quickly, though Sam had yet to decide if that was a good or bad thing. Only six weeks after he'd moved away, Aiden broached the idea of a breakup.

"Better to end it now, while we can still look each other in the eye and be friends," he'd offered.

There had been tears, and the worst fights of all. But eventually Sam had to give in. When Aiden knew he was right he was immovable.

But I don't have to like it.

Another two grey months had passed and springtime was chasing the snow off the

Buffalo streets, but Sam still had mixed feelings. She wanted another option to magically present itself, but every day brought more disillusionment.

Chapter 2 --Hong Kong convention

The next morning at the offices of Morgan Advertising, Sam tried to lose herself in the endless supply of misplaced files, customer contacts, and deadlines. When Uncle Ty blew in midmorning, she was embroiled in negotiating a new contract by e-mail and taking care of six different loose ends in the lapses between messages.

Uncle Ty dropped a plane ticket in front of her. It landed in the only six inches of bare desk there were.

She eyed it like it might turn into a snake at any moment. "No. No no no no no. This is not the best time. No. This is the worst time..." She glared up at him, suspiciously. "You always handle the conferences. Isa got to you, didn't she?"

Uncle Ty put on his innocent face, an unconvincing thing at best. He spread a hand over his heart and said, "I have no idea what you're talking about. I simply think you're ready to handle the... excitement." He shuddered. His lack of enthusiasm for industry conferences was no secret. Sam's guess was that there were not enough single and attractive ladies at them to suit her uncle, or they were there but would have the information necessary to seek revenge upon his business. Either way he tended to find six stupid yet attractive young women to take his mind off the stress once he got back.

But, though Uncle Ty was many things, petty or mean were not among them. He wasn't the type to send Sam on jobs just to avoid them himself.

If even Uncle Ty thinks I'm in a rut maybe things are worse than I want to believe. It takes a lot of concern to push through the layers of hornball.

She sighed and picked up the ticket. The plane left for Hong Kong in a week. She had to admit that the excitement of a week in such an exotic place was kind of tempting. She was still annoyed, but if she was going to be pressured to do things, this was a much better option than another bout of yoga.

The annual Advertising Innovation Convention, though practically useless was a nice feather in the company's cap. Someone had to go, and it seemed like this time it had to be Sam.

Of course, she still wasn't going down without a fight. "I'll need to put in a lot of overtime this week to get ready to be away..." The ticket was in her hand, between them. *I will be damned if I take this on just to please you.*

"Certainly." Uncle Ty's handsome face was serene.

"And the company is going to pay for my expenses while I'm there?"

"Of course. I know I only survive such things by using room service to a scandalizing degree."

"Ok. And now, this is very important so look at me." She took a deep breath, "Uncle Ty, you are absolutely forbidden to have sex on my desk while I'm gone."

He looked briefly pained, then smiled. "For you? Of course."

Sam pocketed the ticket. A convention full of strangers actually sounded like a perfect place to lose herself for a week. The panels didn't actually matter, what mattered was only that the company made an appearance, then they could put *Attended AIC* on their credentials for another year. Customers didn't know how useless it really was. She could go through the motions and then veg out in her hotel room every night, an ocean away from

Aiden and the people who wanted her to forget him.

Uncle Ty grinned. There was a bit of victory in his voice as he continued, "But I make no promises regarding chairs, walls, or other office décor."

Despite herself, Sam laughed a little and threw a file at him. "God! You're a dirty old man!"

His smile was proud, "Damn straight."

For the rest of the day Sam's general levels of irritation were a bit less. When she felt Uncle Ty's concerned gaze rest on her she remembered that Aiden wasn't the only person who's ever loved her. It didn't do much to ease the gaping hole in her heart, but for the first time in a long while she felt less like giving the world a black eye.

Isa came in to pick up their deliveries in the early afternoon. They had met because Isa was a courier for many of the businesses downtown. The first time Isa -- Isabella to Sam at the time -- had stuck around to chat, Sam had been flabbergasted. She'd assumed that the smart, beautiful girl would want nothing to do with her. Now Isa was the best friend Sam had ever had.

When Sam told her about the upcoming trip, Isa was simultaneously excited for her and concerned to have her out of sight for so long. The result was an explosion of energy. "There's so much to do! We have to get you ready!"

"I was just going to use my business suit. And wear my regular clothes during the down times..." But she saw the pleading look on Isa's face.

"Fine. But I am not spending more than two hundred dollars, total." For once she left the office at the same time as Uncle Ty, and let Isa take her shopping for things she didn't really need. *When there's only two people in the world who care,* she figured, *I suppose you'd better humor them.*

Chapter 3 -- Tom the sound guy

Sam got off the plane in Hong Kong in a blur. Her last few days in the States had been a whirlwind of last minute details.

The cat had to be taken care of, things at work needed to be squared away, and all the time there were random things she needed to remember to throw in her bags.

Normally for business trips she drove herself to the airport, or caught a cab, but this time both Isa and Uncle Ty saw her off. It was a bit draining, actually.

Isa teared up and Uncle Ty was full of last minute advice and innuendo. Though Sam was warmed by their attention, she also found it exhausting and felt a bit guilty about how glad she was to leave them behind at boarding.

She took a taxi to the hotel where the convention would be held. She intended to explore before she went home, but for the moment all she wanted was to know where her bed was and take a shower.

It had been the longest flight she'd ever been on; with a layover in Branson, Missouri of all places before flying over the seemingly infinite expanse of the Pacific Ocean. Apparently the flight had been cheap because of the insanity of the flight plan.

At the moment, the lights of the city flashed by without exciting any interest in her.

Thank goodness hotels are the same everywhere, she thought as she checked in. The lady behind the desk spoke English but even if she hadn't the basic check in procedure didn't actually require much communication.

It was 6PM here, and there were only a few events scheduled for the night. Sam's eyes flicked over the convention schedule; she had volunteered to be part of a panel on troubleshooting in a small business environment tomorrow, but tonight there wasn't much she had to do. She decided to show up to see Social Networking: Friend or Foe? but that was it.

An hour later she had settled into her room and taken a shower, deciding afterward that for tonight she didn't care if anyone minded her jeans. Of course, she regretted that decision instantly when she walked into a conference room full of serious faced business suited professionals. *Too late now,* she sat down in the back. A couple of fresh faced people took the stage and began a staged discussion of how to use Facebook to promote your advertising business. Sam yawned.

"Riveting, eh?" a voice dripping with sarcastic laughter whispered behind her. Without thinking about it, Sam nodded. Another yawn prevented her from replying.

A face poked over her shoulder, "Hey, hot stuff. Mind handing me that cable? It's ok, it's not live." Sam nearly fell out of her chair, her surprised squeak earning her some dirty looks from the rows ahead of her.

She turned around to see a tall, scruffy looking young man with his sleeves rolled up past his elbows. He had a tool belt slung low on his slim hips with various technical looking things poking out of the pouches, and facial hair somewhere between a five o'clock shadow and a goatee. There was a hoop in one of his bushy, dark eyebrows. He had laughing, almond shaped eyes.

While Sam gaped, the man swung himself into the seat next to her and picked the cable up himself. He seemed to be splicing it into a different one.

"You here for the duration?" he asked with a gesture that seemed to encompass the hotel and everything in it. His voice was light and somewhat gravelly, with a slight accent that put emphasis in unexpected places.

Sam ventured a nod. "I- I'm here for the convention, yes." To her own ears she sounded like a scared little girl and she tried to compensate by putting on her business voice "And you are?"

He stuck out a moderately grease stained hand, "Tom Wong. Singer, songwriter, musician. And I'm your sound guy for all this," again his airy gesture took in everything about the convention. Sam put her hand in his, and he raised it to his lips.

When she snatched it back he grinned and shrugged.

While talking, Tom was busy wiring two cables together with expert movements of his long fingered hands. As he wrapped electrical tape around the finished product, Sam realized she was completely ignoring what was happening onstage. *Super professional there, girl.*

"Well," Tom said, "Unfortunately I have a lot to get done tonight so I must leave you. But I would love to see *much more* of you soon." He gave her another sweeping look and a mischievous smile, then he straightened up and walked away, leaving through one of the employee doors that blend into the walls and hotel guests are not supposed to notice.

Sam blinked. Her jetlagged brain slowly adding things up. *Was that guy flirting with me?* Luckily, she was fairly familiar with the intricacies of social media because she did not hear a single word of the presentation. Afterward she meandered back to her room and, flinging herself onto the hard bed, fell into a fitful sleep.

Chapter 4 -- Mixed feelings

Uncle Ty was not a big fan of hard work, so Morgan Advertising's contributions to business conventions was always minimal. Sam's panel was a Q&A session where audience members first shared problems they'd encountered in the past and the panel members answered with how they would have handled the situation, followed by the group brainstorming the best solution from everyone's input.

Sam thought the whole thing was pretty useless. *I don't think I've ever had the same problem pop up twice, unless it's Uncle Ty's filing.* But she didn't have to prepare anything, just show up looking nice.

She slept in as late as possible and then put on her new suit. It had been one of the many things Isa had insisted she buy, so now she owned two suits.

Admit it, you're never wearing the old one again, so you still only have one suit.

The new one was much more comfortable and also a lot more attractive. It was navy blue with baby blue pinstripes. It hugged her chest and torso snugly, accentuating her waist before flaring at her hips. With a pair of comfortable heels the outfit made her feel competent and cool, instead of awkward and sad as she usually did lately.

She stepped up to the table on the stage and started to pin the little microphone to her chest. "Here, let me help you with that," Tom stepped close to her and adjusted the mic. He was close enough that she could feel his body heat, his fingers brushed against the fabric of her suit just hard enough to stimulate her skin underneath.

She looked up at him, and his eyes met hers. "So, beautiful stranger, are you going to tell me your name?"

Though he was only asking for her name, his tone was unmistakably seductive. And to her embarrassment and surprise, Sam felt herself responding to it. Heat flooded her and she felt her heart jump. She backed away hastily and tripped over a chair, landing squarely on her butt. A few people nearby tittered, but Tom just smiled and offered her his hand. *He acts like he knocks women down with a smile all the time. Cocky punk.* But she felt a jolt of excitement as his long fingers wrapped around hers and he pulled her to her feet. She stood there, unwilling to release his hand, it felt so good wrapped around hers.

He ducked his head and whispered in her ear, "Let's turn it on, hmm?"

This time he did chuckle as she jumped back, blushing furiously. He pointed to her microphone. "The switch is so small that some people can't find it. Some people even claim it doesn't exist. But," he closed the distance between them again and murmured, "I am very good." He flipped a tiny switch on the back of her mic and stepped off the stage. Sam had just enough time to scramble to her seat as the panelists were announced.

She knew her face was still a little red when the announcer called "Samantha Morgan, Morgan Advertising, USA." At the back of the room she saw Tom wave hugely and silently mouth, "Nice to meet you, Samantha!" before he slipped out the double doors.

Sam fanned her face with a blank paper as the first question was posed. *How does that guy not get fired?* she wondered. *Or arrested for sexual harassment?*

Thoughts of police led her immediately to thoughts of Aiden and the familiar gut punch sense of loss and regret. She was guiltily aware of lingering feelings of arousal and she felt like she was betraying him. *Girl, you are so screwed up.* She flopped her head into her hands and groaned.

"Miss Morgan, are you well? Do you need the first aid team?" The panel announcer, the whole table of panelists and every member of the audience was looking at her. She felt her blush spring back to life and had to choke back another groan.

"I'm fine. Just, um, jet lagged." She sipped from her water glass, wishing it wasn't clear so she could hide behind it. *This is going to be a very long hour and a half...*

By the time the event was over, Sam was mentally exhausted. Her mind kept stubbornly returning to thoughts of Aiden, her feelings of embarrassment, and worst of all the way Tom made her feel when he stood close to her. Normally she could wing a panel like this one easily. This time she had forced herself to write down each question, knowing she'd forget it before her turn to speak if she didn't. As it was she had to bite her tongue to keep from muttering things to herself. Things like "jerk," "oh my god," and "yes." She felt absolutely fried.

She took a shower and lay down naked on the bed. She wished Aiden were here with her. When she felt overwhelmed he could always make her feel better. She let her hands wander over her breasts, relaxing as she imagined him squeezing them. She imagined the taste of his mouth and the feel of his breath on her skin as he kissed her. Her nipples crinkled under her fingers and she pretended it was his mouth that electrified them.

One hand wandered lower, slipping into her womanhood. She imagined long, rough fingers gripping her thighs and probing her as she stroked herself. She teased her nipple, gasping as she pictured white teeth pinching them gently, rough facial hair brushing against her tender flesh. Simultaneously, she fondled the bud inside her cleft, trying to feel the callouses of a manly hand.

As her excitement built, each tiny motion sent bigger and bigger jolts of sensation down her legs and up her spine. She ran her fingers harder and faster through her slick folds, each time they brushed against her sensitive peak she shivered. Moaning, she arched her back, feeling her pleasure reach its breaking point. She bit her lip and cried out as her release washed over her. Throbbing heat radiated out from where her fingers played and she writhed as each wave took her.

As she lay there panting, with little tremors of passion still shooting through her, she wished she wasn't so alone. *I want those long fingers all over me for real... Wait, that's not right.* Aiden had strong, square hands. They weren't soft, but they were definitely not long and rough. And Aiden was always clean shaven. She had been imagining Tom! Embarrassment knotted her stomach and she covered her face with her hands. *What is wrong with me?*

She got off the bed, it felt like she'd cheated on Aiden there and she didn't want to look at it any more. She threw on some clean jeans and a tank top. She definitely didn't want to be in her room for a while, and if she stayed in the hotel and saw Tom? *I think I might spontaneously combust from shame if I see him right now. I need to get out of here.* She decided to go exploring. Maybe even find a present for Isa.

Chapter 5 --EARTHQUAKE!!

Sam was in the Stanley Market, wondering if Isa would prefer a cheongsam or something more touristy as a gift. Ideally, the dress should be tailored, but Isa had a model's figure and it would probably look great on her. *But stores at home carry them too. Maybe she'd prefer some of those scary looking herbs?*

She'd wandered around for several hours. First she had drifted along with the crowd, following the smell of incense to a huge temple with giant incense burners hanging from the ceiling. After that, she hopped onto a tourist bus and got off when she saw a string of little restaurants. She found a place with a line at the door but reasonable prices and when she got a place at the bar she had some of the most delicious dim sum she'd ever tasted. She got a second order to go and then meandered over to the shopping area.

As she contemplated a tiny replica of the enormous Buddha statue that she hadn't managed to find yet, Sam felt the ground shake. *An earthquake? Cool. I never notice them when they happen. I'll have a story to tell when I get back home.*

But then the rumbling came again, stronger, and she saw a number of the shoppers around her looking concerned. Shop owners turned to each other, talking in low urgent tones.

I need to get back to the hotel, Sam decided, trying to bury her growing nervousness under specific action. As she turned toward the bus stop a roar filled her ears, rising from the ground like nothing she had ever heard before. The bucking street threw her to her hands and knees.

I've got to find somewhere safe. People were running in all directions, or trying to at least, most being tossed around every time they stood. A woman stepped right on Sam as she tried to flee and more people were headed towards her. Sam crawled to the side of the street and crouched behind a vendor's overturned table. It did her absolutely no good as the ground seemed to drop out from under everything.

Sam, the table, and thousands of strangers fell six feet, only to be tossed in the air again.

Time slowed. Sam could hear cars crashing somewhere nearby, and screams. The buildings lining the street were all swaying, their windows exploded, and raining glass on the people below. She landed hard, bounced, and hit her head on the shaking pavement. Her vision darkened and she blacked out.

When she woke up, everything around her was dark. Night had fallen and the power was out. Without the brilliant city lights, the pitch blackness was only pierced by an occasional flashlight beam. Sam checked herself, she was sore all over but nothing seemed broken.

And my head is killing me. Her phone had no signal, *big shock there,* but she used the flashlight function to pick her way through the rubble towards the nearest flashlight beam. She was still clutching the paper take-out bag, but the bottom had ripped out and it was empty. She flung it away.

It was being wielded by a man in a safety helmet. Sam had never been in a situation like this before. *I think I'm supposed to ask for help, but I don't think I really need it.* "Sir? Could you tell me which direction the Marriott is in?"

"Wait over there." His flashlight beam swept over to an emergency vehicle. A crowd of dirty, wide-eyed people crowded silently around it. Some had shock blankets wrapped around their shoulders.

"But I-"

"Over there!" he snapped. *Jeez, way to be the calm, reassuring rescuer there, dude. But I suppose we're all having a bad day.* Too dazed to argue or come up with an alternate plan, Sam joined the throng of waiting people. *I guess I'm just one more victim. Lame.*

She waited for an hour, watching as more and more people joined the silent group. Nobody spoke. Occasionally a siren and commotion would announce that another person had been found, one with severe enough injuries to need immediate removal to a hospital. Sam found herself growing irrationally jealous of them. *I am so close to just walking away from here. I think*

I could retrace my steps. But my battery is low.

Even after a blow to the head, she wasn't quite willing to trust that she could navigate a strange city in pitch blackness. *I wonder what I have to do to get one of those blankets?*

She sat down and watched through slitted eyes as another flashlight beam approached. The way the light flared she couldn't tell if the person behind it was an emergency worker or another victim come to join the herd.

Actually, it was neither. "Samantha?" Tom's voice called. The beam panned over the crowd and stopped on her face.

She flinched away, the light was blinding after so much dark. "Hey!"

"Samantha! Thank goodness! Are you hurt? I knew I'd find you." He knelt next to Sam, his brows furrowed in concern, but he had a little crooked smile, too. A familiar face, one that didn't look as lost as she felt, flooded Sam with joy. She flung her arms around him, giggling stupidly. He held her gently, petting her back and repeating, "Hey there, easy..." until she could talk again.

He pulled her up and led her away. None of the victims or emergency people said anything or tried to stop them. Hand in hand, they slowly navigated the shattered, black city. Occasionally he would pick out a shop or an alleyway with his flashlight beam and tell her a story about the place. This was the place he won his first fight. That was where he used to practice guitar. That was the bar he went to after shows; that one was completely destroyed and Tom insisted on a moment of silence for it.

Sam watched his face. *His whole home is basically gone. Sane people are in shock, or crying, or angry. How is he making jokes?*

Chapter 6 -- Together with Tom

Dawn was breaking when they finally reached the hotel. The lobby was quiet, but a number of people were asleep on the couches and chairs, and a few on the floor. They passed the sleepers silently and went up to Sam's room.

The furniture was knocked all over, and the mirror was broken, but the bed was fine and they both sat down on it. Sam had taken some Ibuprofen and used the ice pack from Tom's first aid kit as they walked, but hadn't wanted to slow down long enough to check for anything else.

Now, Tom helped her wash off the scrapes on her hands. "You really were lucky this was the worst you got." Sam nodded; she guessed there were people who had not survived, let alone with just a bump and a few scrapes. She hissed as the alcohol burned her raw palms, and he instantly stopped to stroke her cheek. "Sorry," he whispered.

Sam felt the rising excitement Tom provoked in her. She remembered the last time she'd been on this bed, when it had been Tom in her fantasy, not Aiden. And Tom had come to save her. He'd noticed she was gone before the earthquake hit, and had searched each tourist trap in turn until he found her. Her heart pounded in her chest as his enormous hands wrapped tenderly around her shoulders.

She looked into his face, eyes wide. Keeping her eyes locked on his, she laid a hand on his cheek, and trailed her thumb across his lower lip. It was warm and dry. She saw excitement light his eyes at her touch. "Tom, thank you for coming to get me." Her voice was low and husky, she hardly recognized it.

He bent his head, until his lips were just centimeters from hers. His deep breath ruffled her bangs. He must have borrowed her mouthwash because he smelled like spearmint. Then, as if reaching a decision, his arms encircled her and he kissed her. Sam marveled that a man so full of himself could be so tender. His every move was so gentle that even her aching body registered only pleasure. He helped her slowly remove her shirt, and unclasped her bra with a deft movement, freeing her full, ivory white breasts.

Sam reveled in the newness of him. After the events of the night she trusted him absolutely, but every inch of him was new and exciting. She traced his collarbone and his hard jawline, tasting his salt sweat. He took her mouth in his and he tasted sweet. His hands explored her body softly but his tongue was fierce, it blazed into her mouth ravenously.

Get your own copy now of "*REBOUND LOVE*" to continue reading about Samantha's adventures in love.

Denise Daniella Darcy

Dear Reader,

We hope you enjoyed this adventure-in-love story.

Make sure you don't miss out on new and exciting stories by our romance writer Triple D. Join our Preferred Customer list to stay in touch. You will get:

1. *Advance notice of new stories in the series*
2. *Special deals for preferred customers only*
3. *Flash news*

Sign up now at:

http://www.denisedanielladarcy.com/newsletter

Cheers,

Sally Carruthers, *Triple D's Helper*

Also by Denise Daniella Darcy

Samantha's LOVE & ROMANCE Series

First Love – Book 1

Rebound Love – Book 2

Cowboy Love – Book 3

Casual Love – Book 4

Hi Readers, Denise here. I am busy writing more stories about Samantha's adventures in love so check my website **www.DeniseDaniellaDarcy.com** for the most up-to-date list. Happy reading! *DDD*

First Love

Other Titles By Durango Publishing Corp.®

Denise Daniella Darcy

Recommended Reads

If you liked *FIRST LOVE*, check out these other great stories by popular authors.

<u>Not Quite Dating (Not Quite series)</u>, Catherine Bybee

<u>Tempting Her Best Friend (A What Happens in Vegas Novel)</u>, Gina Maxwell

<u>Night Moves</u>, Nora Roberts

<u>Melt For Him (a Fighting Fire novel)</u>, Lauren Blakely

<u>Midnight Betrayal</u>, Melinda Leigh

About Denise Daniella Darcy

Denise Daniella Darcy, or Triple D as she is affectionately called by family, friends and fans, started life as a mortician's helper. Faced with the daily task of making the dead appear happy, she decided to switch careers and apply her talents to making the living happy instead. She achieves that through her Love & Romance novels. She writes from the heart, with a viewpoint that to grow you need to push your boundaries and you find happiness wherever it may appear and in any shape that it comes.

Triple D writes stimulating contemporary romances with passion, humor and a down to earth feel that resonates with her readers. She creates the 'I can't put the book down, just 1 more page before I turn out the lights' stories that keep you interested, engaged and involved.

Denise lives a vibrant and enthusiastic life on the west coast with a full house, including her children, cats and dogs, assorted critters, and her own personal hunk of a husband. The coffee is always on, the table always full of family and friends, and a spirited discussion is underway. And when evening rolls around, often enough a party is sent out to raid the wine cellar. Lively, fun and full of life.

Her novels include FIRST LOVE, REBOUND LOVE, COWBOY LOVE and CASUAL LOVE. This fall Triple D is releasing a new series in the young adult and teen romance genre.

To receive an email when Triple D releases a new novel, get on our newsletter at:
http://www.denisedanielladarcy.com/newsletter

And I know she'd love you to visit her at www.DeniseDaniellaDarcy.com.

Dear Reader,

One final note. Thank you so much for reading this story. I hope you really liked it.

As you probably know, many people look at the reviews on Amazon before they decide to purchase a book.

If you liked the book, could you please take a minute to leave a 4 or 5 star review with your feedback?

You can do that right here at: http://www.amazon.com/First-Love-Samanthas-Romance-romance-ebook/dp/B00O66VR92

60 seconds is all I am asking you for, and it would mean the world to me. Your friendly help will certainly help me in further research & writing.

Thank you so much, and here's to happy reading.

Triple D

Denise Daniella Darcy

PS. *Don't forget to get your* **FREE ALTERNATE ENDINGS** *here:*

http://www.denisedanielladarcy .com/firstlovealternates

Just my way of giving you something extra and thanking you for reading my books.

www.ingramcontent.com/pod-product-compliance
Lightning Source LLC
Chambersburg PA
CBHW070927130626
46555CB00001B/326